That's
She Said

Eileen Ulick   &   Willie B. Hardigan

That's What She Said

"IF YOU'RE JUST GOING TO HAVE ONE, YOU MIGHT AS WELL MAKE IT STIFF"

THAT'S WHAT SHE SAID

"IT DOESN'T LOOK THAT BIG ON CAMERA BUT I TAKE PRIDE IN IT"

THAT'S WHAT SHE SAID

"IT WAS SO SMALL I BARELY FELT IT IN MY MOUTH"

THAT'S WHAT SHE SAID

"I'VE GOT TWO IN THE BACK AND ONE IN THE FRONT"

THAT'S WHAT SHE SAID

"DON'T
WORRY,
I'LL GET
THE BALLS"

THAT'S WHAT SHE SAID

"DANG, THESE HOLES ARE SO CLOSE TOGETHER"

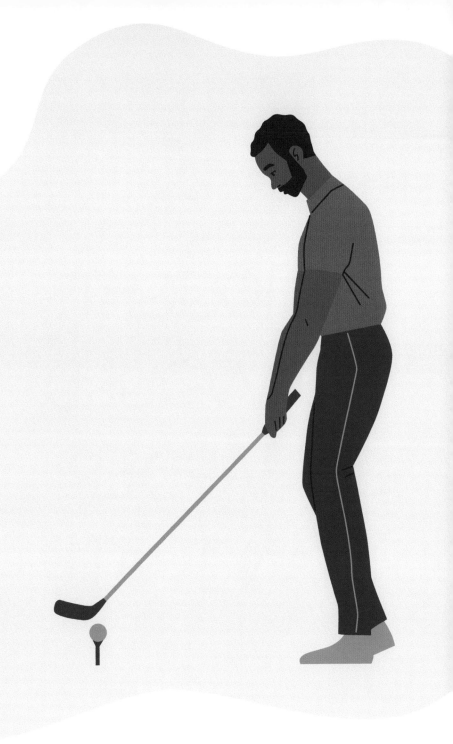

THAT'S WHAT SHE SAID

"I THOUGHT YOU WOULD BE HARDER THAN THAT"

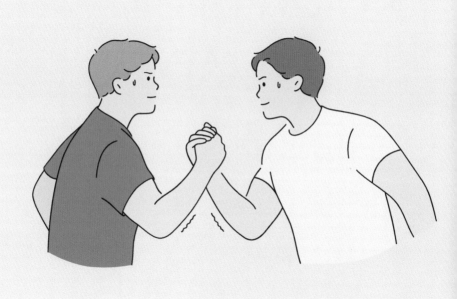

THAT'S WHAT SHE SAID

"I DIDN'T KNOW YOU HAD TO GROW A GIANT BUSH BEFORE YOU COULD GET ANY"

THAT'S WHAT SHE SAID

"THAT IS
THE TINIEST
PACKAGE
EVER"

THAT'S WHAT SHE SAID

"I NEED SOMETHING NICE AND BIG. I'VE BEEN CRAVING IT ALL DAY"

THAT'S WHAT SHE SAID

"THAT PUMP WAS FASTER THAN I EXPECTED"

THAT'S WHAT SHE SAID

"I DON'T
THINK I
CAN LAST
MUCH
LONGER"

THAT'S WHAT SHE SAID

"YOU GOTTA LET THAT THING HANG SO IT DOESN'T STIFFEN UP"

THAT'S WHAT SHE SAID

"I STILL HAVE SOME ON MY FACE FROM EARLIER"

THAT'S WHAT SHE SAID

"DAMN IT! WHY WON'T IT STAY UP"

THAT'S WHAT SHE SAID

"FOUR STROKES IS ABOUT ALL I CAN HANDLE RIGHT NOW"

THAT'S WHAT SHE SAID

"THESE ARE ALL SO STRANGELY SHAPED"

THAT'S WHAT SHE SAID

"GIVE ME ANOTHER SMALL ONE TO HOLD ON TO"

THAT'S WHAT SHE SAID

"JUST WAIT UNTIL YOU SEE THE DOWNSTAIRS"

THAT'S WHAT SHE SAID

"I TOTALLY DIDN'T EXPECT IT TO GET THAT BIG"

THAT'S WHAT SHE SAID

"THIS IS
GOING TO
BE QUICK
AND EASY"

THAT'S WHAT SHE SAID

"ITS SO HARD FOR ME TO KEEP THIS THING UP"

THAT'S WHAT SHE SAID

"THIS
DOESN'T
FEEL LIKE
A LARGE"

THAT'S WHAT SHE SAID

"I ONLY TAKE BIG LOADS"

THAT'S WHAT SHE SAID

"YEAH, THAT WAS OVER WAY TOO FAST"

THAT'S WHAT SHE SAID

"THAT THING WAS DEEPER THAN I EXPECTED"

THAT'S WHAT SHE SAID

"YOU JUST HAVE TO USE YOUR FIST TO BREAK IT IN"

THAT'S WHAT SHE SAID

"I WOULDN'T
WANT IT
ANY
BIGGER"

THAT'S WHAT SHE SAID

"I HOPE I DON'T BUST A BUNCH OF TIMES"

THAT'S WHAT SHE SAID

"I FEEL LIKE I'VE BEEN SO TIGHT LATELY"

THAT'S WHAT SHE SAID

"GETTING IT
IN IS A
WHOLE
OTHER ISSUE
FOR ME"

THAT'S WHAT SHE SAID

"THAT CAME OUT WAY TOO FAST! I DIDN'T WANT THAT MUCH"

THAT'S WHAT SHE SAID

"I DON'T THINK IT'S GOING TO FIT NO MATTER WHAT YOU DO"

THAT'S WHAT SHE SAID

"THERE'S A LOT OF GROWTH ON IT! I'M EXCITED"

THAT'S WHAT SHE SAID

"IT'S JUST TOO MUCH BLOWING FOR ME"

THAT'S WHAT SHE SAID

"DO YOU NEED HELP GETTING IT UP?"

THAT'S WHAT SHE SAID

15610414R00045